Story play™

This book belongs to

_____ .

This book was read by

_____

on

_____ .

Are you ready to start reading the **StoryPlay** way?

Read the story on its own. Play the activities together
as you read!

Ready. Set. Smart!

For Maud, Milly, and Ben — T.M.

For Sarah, with love — G.P-R.

First published in Great Britain in 2002 by Orchard Books London
First American edition 2002 published by Orchard Books

Library of Congress Cataloging-in-Publication Data available
ISBN 978-1-338-11536-9
10 9 8 7 6 5 4 3 2 1   17 18 19 20 21
Printed in Guang Dong Province, China   154
This edition first printing, January 2017
Book design by Doan Buu

Dinosaurumpus!

by Tony Mitton

illustrated by Guy Parker-Rees

Cartwheel Books
An Imprint of Scholastic Inc.

There's a quake and a quiver
and a rumbling around.

It makes you shiver.
It's a thundery sound.

"Shake, shake, shudder...
near the sludgy old swamp.
The dinosaurs are coming.
Get ready to romp.

Donk!

Donk!

Donk!

Here's **Triceratops** jumping UP and DOWN doing dinosaur hops.

Can you point to and count Triceratops's three horns?

Watch out for
Deinosuchus
with her
snip-snap grin,
as she perches
on her tail and
twists
in a spin.

Does Deinosuchus remind you
of another animal that is still alive today?
(Here's a clue: It starts with the letter
A and loves swamps!)

Apatosaurus stops
for a slushy, mushy snack.
His tail starts swinging with a

Thwack! Thwack! Thwack!

"Shake, shake, shudder...
near the sludgy swamp.
The dinosaurs are coming.
Get ready to romp.

Pteranodon dives with a swift, sharp swoop. He shrieks out an

Eeeeeek! as he swirls in a loop.

Stegosaurus stomps along
with lots of her playmates.

Clatter! Clatter! Clatter!

go their bony
back plates.

"Shake, shake, shudder...
near the sludgy old swamp.
The dinosaurs are coming.
Get ready to romp.

Styracosaurus shakes
his collar and his spikes.
Rattle! Rattle! Rattle!
is the noise that he likes!

A pack of **Deinonychuses**
go running by fast—
with a Zoom! Zoom! Zoom!
so they won't be the last.

"Shake, shake, shudder...
near the sludgy old swamp.
The dinosaurs are coming.
Get ready to romp.

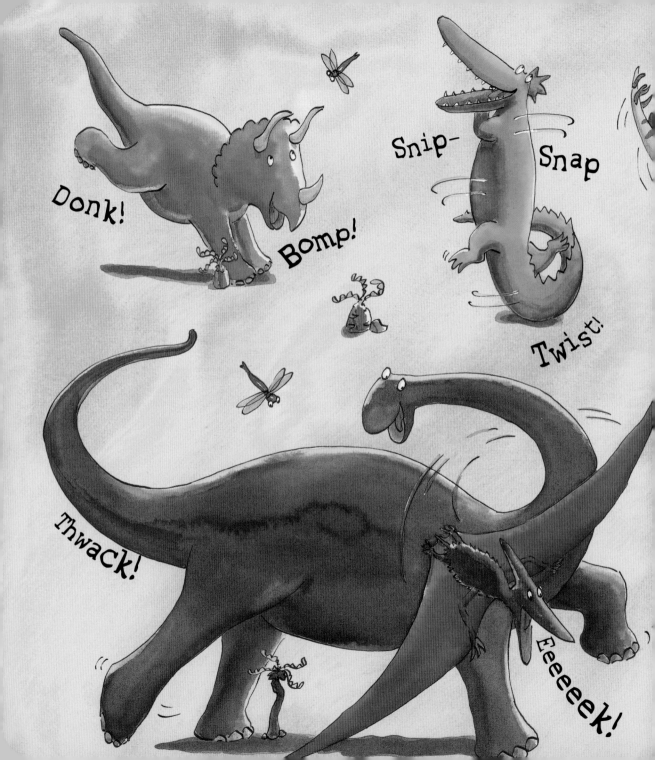

Clatter!

How well do you remember the dinosaurs' names? Point to these four dinos:

- Stegosaurus
  (Hint: I have back plates.)
- Pteranodon
  (Hint: I have wings.)
- Apatosaurus
  (Hint: I have a long neck.)
- Deinonychus
  (Hint: I run on two legs.)

Rattle!

Zoom! Zoom!

Come and take a peek . . .

"Shake, shake, shudder . . .
near the sludgy old swamp.
Everybody's doing the
dinosaur romp.

He's huge
and he's heavy,

but all he wants to do . . .

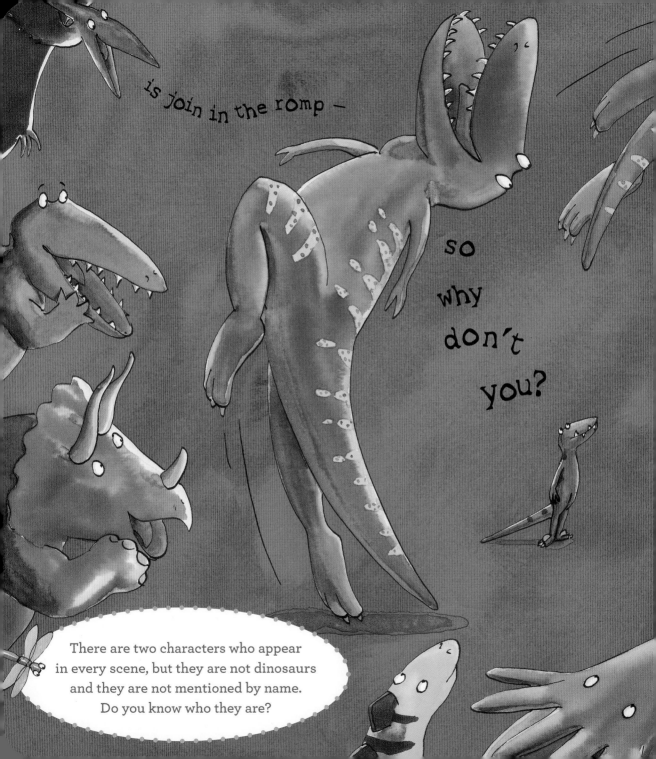

Get romping with **T. rex**
and STOMP! STOMP! STOMP!
Wave your arms madly.

make your feet go Bomp!

rumpus!

"Shake, shake, shudder...
near the sludgy old swamp.
Everybody's doing the
dinosaur romp.

It makes you want to shout,

jump, jiggle, and sing.

"Shake, shake, shudder...
near the sludgy old swamp.
Everybody's doing the
dinosaur romp.

The words *SING* and *ZING* rhyme. Can you think of other words that rhyme with them?

But soon all the rompers grow sleepy and slow.

The rumpus calms down and the sound drops low.

The rompers drift together
and tumble in a heap . . .

'til finally the dinosaurs
are all fast asleep.

And now the only noise
in the deep of the night
is . . .

dinosaur-snoring
'til the next day's light.

Story time fun never ends with these creative activities!

★ Boogie Woogie! ★

The dinosaurs love to dance so much they made up their very own dance — the Dinosaurumpus. Now it's time to create YOUR own dance! Use these helpful prompts to guide you!

1. Name your dance.
2. Does it have a song? If so, how does it go?
3. Make up your dance. Here are some dance moves to get you started: clapping; stomping; shaking your bottom, legs, or arms; twirling around; jumping up and down.

Now see how many family members and friends you can get to learn the song and dance and perform it together!

★ Rats-o-rumpus! ★

The secret characters that appear in every scene but are never mentioned are rats. What do you think their story is? Are they brother and sister? Best friends? What are their names? Where do they live?

Draw a picture that tells the story of these two rats and what you think happens to them!

★ Dino-love ★

What is your favorite dinosaur and why? Draw a picture of your favorite extinct creature and ask an adult to help you write down why you love it so much. Then hang it up somewhere special!